e Time-for-bed Angel

To my two sons, Josiah and James R.S.

For Fiona Hobdell, to whom we owe so much K.S.

A Lion Children's Book
an imprint of
Lion Hudson plc
Wilkinson House, Jordan Hill Road,
Oxford OX2 8DR, England
www.lionhudson.com
ISBN 978 0 7459 6066 1

First edition 2008
1 3 5 7 9 10 8 6 4 2 0

A catalogue record for this book is available
from the British Library

Typeset in 22/27 Old Claude
Printed and bound in China

The Time-for-bed Angel

Ronica Stromberg
Illustrated by Kristina Stephenson

LION CHILDREN'S

Andrew could ruffle the feathers of an angel.

And he did.

His guardian angel, Sam, could hardly fly fast enough to keep up with his mischief.

And the mess he had to sort out.

Oh, the mess.

At last it was evening.

'Time for bed,' said Andrew's mother.

'Oh, can't I stay up a little longer?' moaned Andrew.

Sam shook his head and went on sorting out another muddle Andrew had left behind.

Andrew went to
brush his teeth.

He squeezed out
the toothpaste...

...and brushed and brushed and brushed.

'Into bed,' said Andrew's mother. She kissed him goodnight, flicked off the light and left Andrew to enjoy sweet dreams.

Phew!

'Just a minute,' said Andrew, jumping up. 'My socks. I need my time-for-bed socks.'

And he began burrowing under his bed to find them.

'What have we left down there?' muttered Sam.

And while Andrew tugged his favourite socks on,
Sam tried to sort things out.

'Now I need my friends in the right order,' said Andrew.

And he began to arrange his cuddly toys from smallest to biggest along his pillow.

Oh dear!

'Where's Bear?' cried Andrew. 'I can't sleep without Bear!'

And he began rummaging through his box of toys.

Poor Sam was quite overwhelmed.

'Bear!' exclaimed Andrew. 'How did I ever lose you? Poor old Bear!'

He gave his cuddly friend a hug and yawned. 'Time for bed, Bear.'

'Time for bed, Andrew,' whispered Sam.
'Come on! Don't fall asleep on the floor.'

At last Andrew was safely lying down.

Sam tucked the quilt around him and sank onto the bed.

Then he heard a sound sweeter than any a choir of angels could sing.

ZZZZZZZZZZZZZZZZZZZZ

Other titles from Lion Children's Books

Safely through the Night *Elena Pasquali & Dubravka Kolanovic*

Angel Shoes *Emily Pound & Sanja Rescek*

Junkyard Dragon *Beth Webb & Russell Julian*